Aussie Native Plants A–Z

Written by Joey Farrell
Illustrated by Jocelyn Gibson

BOOLARONG PRESS
Established 1976

We acknowledge the Traditional Owners of the land on which we publish books,
the Quandamooka people and pay our respects to Elders, past, present and future.

Published by
Boolarong Press
38/1631 Wynnum Road
Tingalpa Qld 4173
Australia.
www.boolarongpress.com.au

First published 2023

A catalogue record for this book is available from the National Library of Australia

ISBN: 9781922643551 (hardback)

Printed and bound in China by Everbest Printing Investment Ltd

I dedicate this book to my mum Jan and my daughter Chloe.
Sharing time in nature with each of you is
one of my favourite things to do.

We acknowledge the Traditional Custodians of the land this book was written on, the Wallumedegal Peoples and neighbouring Clans on Wallumetta Land, as well as the people and land this book was illustrated on, the Tommeginer Peoples of North-West Tasmania. We pay our respects to Elders past, present and emerging.

Find the Country you're living on via the AIATSIS Indigenous map of Australia.

Within these pages, you'll find out about a few of Australia's beautiful, interesting and useful native plants.

They've grown and adapted over thousands of years to live harmoniously with Australia's land, climate, animals and First Nations Peoples.

These plants have some astonishingly unique gifts and purposes that are not found in any other plants, anywhere in the world.

Please remember, even though some are edible, never taste or eat a plant unless you're with an adult who knows a lot about them.

A note about plant names

There are over 250 First Nations languages in Australia, and in some languages, the names of plants can change across the seasons and locations. I encourage you to look up the local language names of your favourite plants.

A is for Angophora costata

The proud Angophora stands tall and strong.
Living along the eastern coast,
Its smooth red trunk is a sight to see
For the visiting animals it hosts.

Come and sit under its cooling branches,
You'll want to stay for hours,
As cockatoos perch on its crooked arms
And the bees buzz in its flowers.

Also known as: Sydney red gum, rusty gum and smooth-barked apple tree
Did you know? Angophora Costata is a gum tree, but not a eucalyptus.

Here's the ancient Boab,
Australia's only type of this tree.
It arrived thousands of years ago,
No-one knows how that came to be.

Found in far north-west Australia,
It carries some incredible tales,
Like how its wide trunks offer shelter,
And were once even used as gaols.

Also known as: boaboa, bottle tree, upside-down tree, and larragadi (in Nyulnyulan language)
Did you know? There are two famous Boab prison trees believed to be over 1,500 years old, with large hollow trunks that are 14 metres around. Boab tree seedpods are a delicious bush food when prepared properly. Look up the Dreaming story about why it looks upside-down, short and wide.

C is for Callistemon

The lovely local Callistemon
Is a pretty common sight,
Flaunting its best in springtime
When its flowers always delight.

They look like little brushes
And come in so many shades.
Their nectar is also delicious
And can be enjoyed in different ways.

Also known as: bottlebrush, and birdak (in Noongar language)
Did you know? Birds love the taste of the Callistemon's nectar, and humans can have it too! As a bush food, you can either suck on the flowers or soak them in water to make a sweet drink. Although, before ever tasting a flower, make sure you check with a grown-up who knows lots about them.

D is for Desert Pea

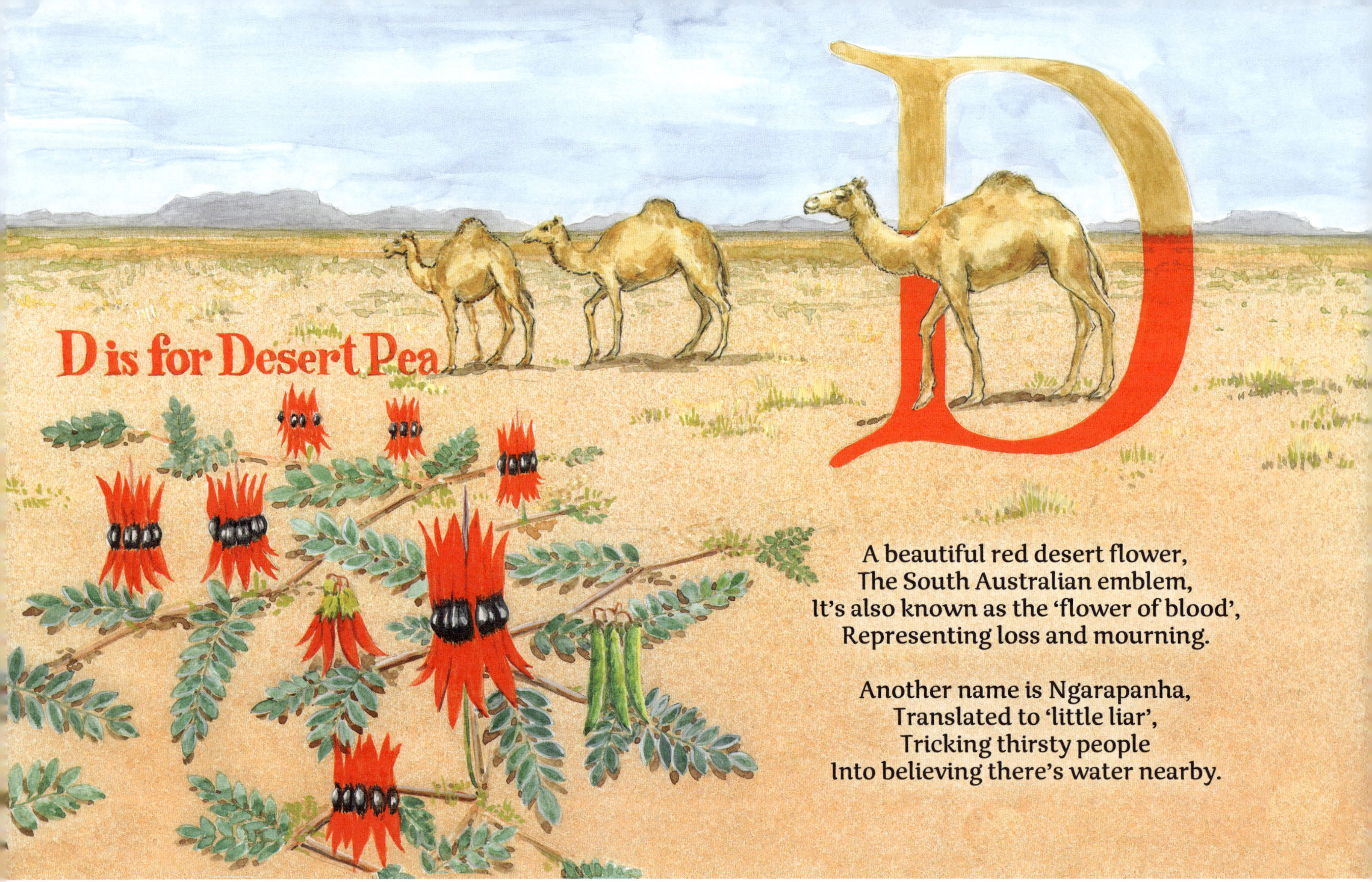

A beautiful red desert flower,
The South Australian emblem,
It's also known as the 'flower of blood',
Representing loss and mourning.

Another name is Ngarapanha,
Translated to 'little liar',
Tricking thirsty people
Into believing there's water nearby.

Also known as: Swainsona formosa, Sturt's desert pea, and ngarapanha (in Adnyamathanha language)
Did you know? There are Dreaming stories about the legend of the Desert Pea, explaining how the soil and the flower got their red colour and the lakes became salty.

E is for Emu Bush

Found in arid areas
With its tolerance to harsh climate,
It's considered sacred and mystical
And part of many animals' diet.

With juicy fruit that emus eat,
That's how it got its name.
It has lots of medical uses
Like healing skin complaints.

Also known as: poverty bush, dogwood, eremophila, native plum, varti-varka (in Adnyamathanha language)
Did you know? There are many different types of Emu Bush and not all of them are eaten by emus. They can look very different too. Emu Bush has different ceremonial and medicinal uses and its leaves have very strong antibacterial properties.

Here's the interesting Finger Lime,
A native Australian citrus.
Growing in northern New South Wales,
Its fruit is quite delicious.

The pulp looks just like fish eggs,
Tasting fresh and tart and sweet.
It's also bursting with vitamin C
And is great bush food to eat.

F is for Finger Lime

Also known as: Citrus australasica, and gulalung (in Bundjalung language)
Did you know? The Finger Lime tree is quite rare because early settlers destroyed many of them when clearing land for farming. It's been used as food and medicine (as an antiseptic) by Australia's First Nations Peoples for thousands of years and can still be found in national parks and private land. Many top chefs love cooking with the Finger Lime.

G is for Gymea Lily

The iconic Gymea
Looks upward toward the sky.
While the luscious leaves stay on the ground,
Its flowering head grows high.

Its Greek name means 'spear'
Thanks to its long thin shape.
As bush food, its flowers are roasted
And the roots made into a cake.

Also known as: Doryanthes excelsa, flame lily, giant lily and giant spear lily

Did you know? The name Gymea comes from the Eora people, and the Sydney suburb Gymea is named after it. The lily can be used for more than food – the fibres from its leaves can be used to make brushes and matting. There's a Dreaming story about the Gymea lily explaining how the plant can quench thirst, provide food and be used as a rope.

H

H is for Happy Wanderer

A purple vine so beautiful,
Like in a fairy palace,
It kisses trees and fence lines
With its smiling flower face.

A haven for native butterflies,
With petals like violet peas,
Its leaves can be crushed and boiled up
To make sweet smelling teas.

Also known as: hardenbergia, false sarsaparilla and coral pea
Did you know? Happy Wanderer can regrow from its roots after fire. The roots were experimented with by early settlers as a substitute for sarsaparilla (a type of drink).

I is for Ironbark Tree

The Ironbark is strong and tall,
One of many eucalypt species.
It can survive blazing bushfires
With its heatproof properties.

The wood's as tough as nails,
Used for building, tools and weapons,
And the oil from its leaves
Can be used for medicine.

Also known as: eucalyptus, grey ironbark, and yirrip (in Kulin language)
Did you know? The bark is resistant to fire and heat and can protect the living tissue inside the trunk.

J is for Native Jasmine

The wild and wonderful Jasmine
Offers a unique scent that's so dear,
Bushwalking in early summer
Your nose will know it's near.

Its common name means 'gift from God'
Because the flowers smell so sweet.
It climbs up trees and fences
And drops black seeds at your feet.

Also known as: Jasminum suavissimum
Did you know? It's thought that the name Jasmine comes from the Persian word 'Yasamin', which means 'gift from God'.

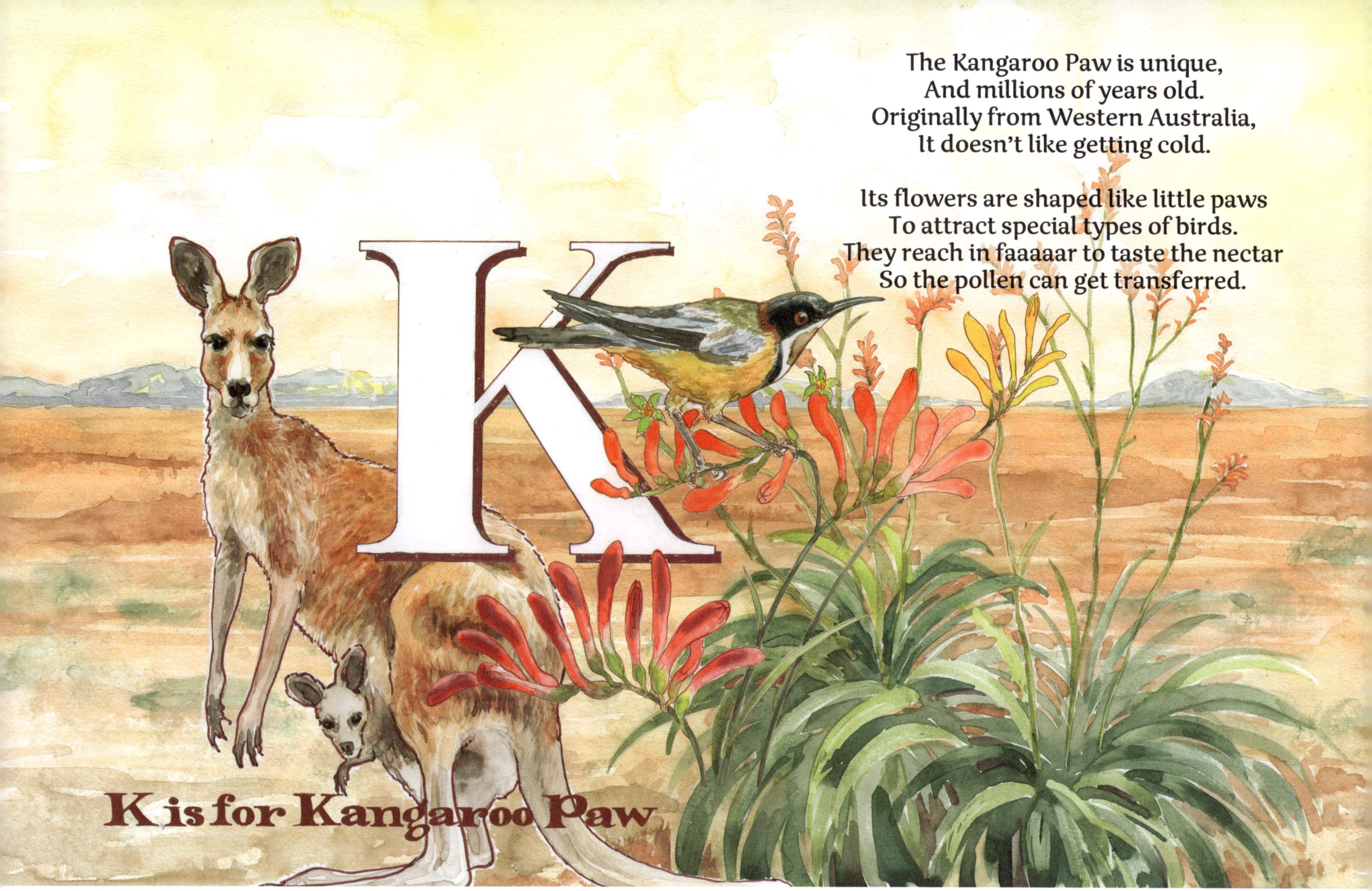

K is for Kangaroo Paw

The Kangaroo Paw is unique,
And millions of years old.
Originally from Western Australia,
It doesn't like getting cold.

Its flowers are shaped like little paws
To attract special types of birds.
They reach in faaaaar to taste the nectar
So the pollen can get transferred.

Also known as: nollamara, kurulbrang and yonga marra, depending on the type (in Nyoongar language)
Did you know? Like many Australian native plants, Kangaroo Paw's roots are so far underground that if a fire comes through, they can grow again really quickly. Kangaroo Paws are also used in preparing traditional medicine.

L is for Lomandra

It's not the most beautiful plant in this book,
But probably one of the most useful.
Its seeds can be used to make damper,
But its starch is even more crucial.

From the base of the leaves, its starch can be chewed
For energy and rehydration,
And the leaves can be used to make baskets and more,
Old lessons passed to a new generation.

Also known as: spiny-head mat-rush, spiky-headed mat-rush, basket grass
Did you know? Lomandra roots can also be used as medicine for insect bites. This plant also exists in other parts of the world and is often seen along highways.

M is for Macadamia

Macadamias are delicious nuts
Grown on a once very rare tree.
Most Macadamias in the world
Originate from a town called Gympie.

Before the early settlers came,
Macadamias were a yummy delicacy,
Their hard shell cracked on a special stone
And offered as gifts in ceremony.

Also known as: baphal (in Yugambeh language)
Did you know? Macadamias originated 60,000 years ago, and some argue they're a seed, not a nut. Look up the Dreaming story 'The legend of Baphal', which explains the history of the Macadamia.

Another delicious bush food,
This one's got a bit of a zing.
The leaves and berries can be used
As a spice or flavouring.

Traditionally it was also used
To fix colic and upset tums,
As well as ground down to a paste
To treat sore teeth and gums.

N is for Native Pepper

Also known as: mountain pepper, Tasmannia lanceolata, pepperberry and pepperleaf
Did you know? A tonic made from the berries, leaves and bark was also used by early settlers to treat scurvy. And the flowers are edible too!

O is for Old Man's Beard

An interesting native plant
That can cling and climb everywhere,
Like rainforests, plains or rocky outcrops
While looking like facial hair.

The beards are funny wispy things
Attached to the fruiting flower.
While not the prettiest plant in town,
It's definitely one to admire.

Also known as: Clematis aristate, traveller's joy and goatsbeard
Did you know? Old Man's Beard branches were used like string or laces by some early settlers.
There are more than 300 species worldwide, and six are native to Australia.

P is for Paperbark

Have you ever tried to strip
The soft bark from this tree
To discover ants crawling underneath?
There's even more to this beauty, you'll see.

The bark has been used for thousands of years
In ways that are quite ingenious,
Including wrapping meat for cooking
And roofing for shelter or *midja.*

Also known as: melaleuca, punk tree, and tjoodah (in Kungarakan language)
Did you know? Paperbark trunks can hold water, and can be cut and bled if you're dehydrated. The leaves and bark can be used as swaddles for babies and to treat things like cuts – the leaves provide antibacterial protection, while the bark can wrap the cut.

Q is for Quandong

A fruit growing desert tree
That doesn't mind a drought,
With fruit full of vitamin C
And seeds you wouldn't be without.

The seed is full of oil
That can be lit and used as light.
Collect it from emu poo
To help you see at night.

Also known as: native peach, desert peach, Santalum acuminatum, and kawantha (in Ngiyampaa language)
Did you know? Fossilised Quandongs have been discovered that are 40 million years old! There are so many uses for this amazing tree and not enough space to list them all.

R is for Rose Mallee

A beautiful shrub from Moora,
But now sadly very rare.
It needs to be protected ASAP
Before it disappears into thin air.

The heart-shaped leaf and rosy flowers
Are so beautiful to see,
Attracting bees and birds alike.
Stay with us, wild Rose Mallee.

Also known as: eucalyptus rhodantha and rose gum
Did you know? The Rose Mallee is listed as vulnerable and rare. This is mainly because of land clearing, uncontrolled fires and weeds.

The salt plains or the ocean
Is usually where salt is harvested.
But why would you bother with that
When you can use these shrubs instead?

The Saltbush leaves can wrap food
To make a salty cooking bed.
Its seeds can also be ground right down
To add flavour to your bread.

S is for Saltbush

Also known as: Atriplex nummularia, Old Man Saltbush, and binga (in Noongar language)
Did you know? When land was cleared by early settlers, much of the Saltbush was removed. This affected the ecosystem! Saltbush is great at absorbing salt from the soil, so when it was removed, there was too much salt in the soil for other plants to survive. People are now replanting Saltbush because they realise removing it was a mistake.

T is for Trigger Plants

The flowers of these amazing plants
Act like a jack in a box.
They attract bugs in for a drink
And out a column pops.

It stamps pollen on their back
So when they fly away,
They'll pollinate other Trigger Plants
In exactly the same way.

Also known as: stylidium

Did you know? These beautiful plants are herbs and can be really tiny. The column is a long stem hiding under the flower — it can stamp pollen on an insect, as well as remove pollen the insect is carrying from another Trigger Plant. They have one of the fastest movements in the plant kingdom, but once the column pops up, it takes about 15 minutes to reset.

U is for Umbrella Bush

This shrub is found around the centre
Of Australia's red desert plains,
Growing at bases of sand dunes
Or near usually dry salt lakes.

There are witchety grubs at its roots,
And the seeds can be ground and eaten,
Made into a sweet type of porridge,
While its leaves can make medicine.

Also known as: sandhill wattle, Acacia ligulata, dune wattle and small coobah
Did you know? The Umbrella Bush leaves and bark can be used to treat colds, chest infections and general illnesses.

V is for Native Violet

A pretty and small plant
That covers over ground,
It can be used instead of grass,
Under trees and shade it's found.

Flowers can be eaten raw,
You could decorate a cake,
Or add them to a salad
Or even put them on a steak.

Also known as: ivy-leaved violet, Viola hederacea and Viola banksii
Did you know? Native Violets are found mostly in south-eastern Australia. Their stems join up to each other to form a type of mat under the leaves.

W is for Waratah

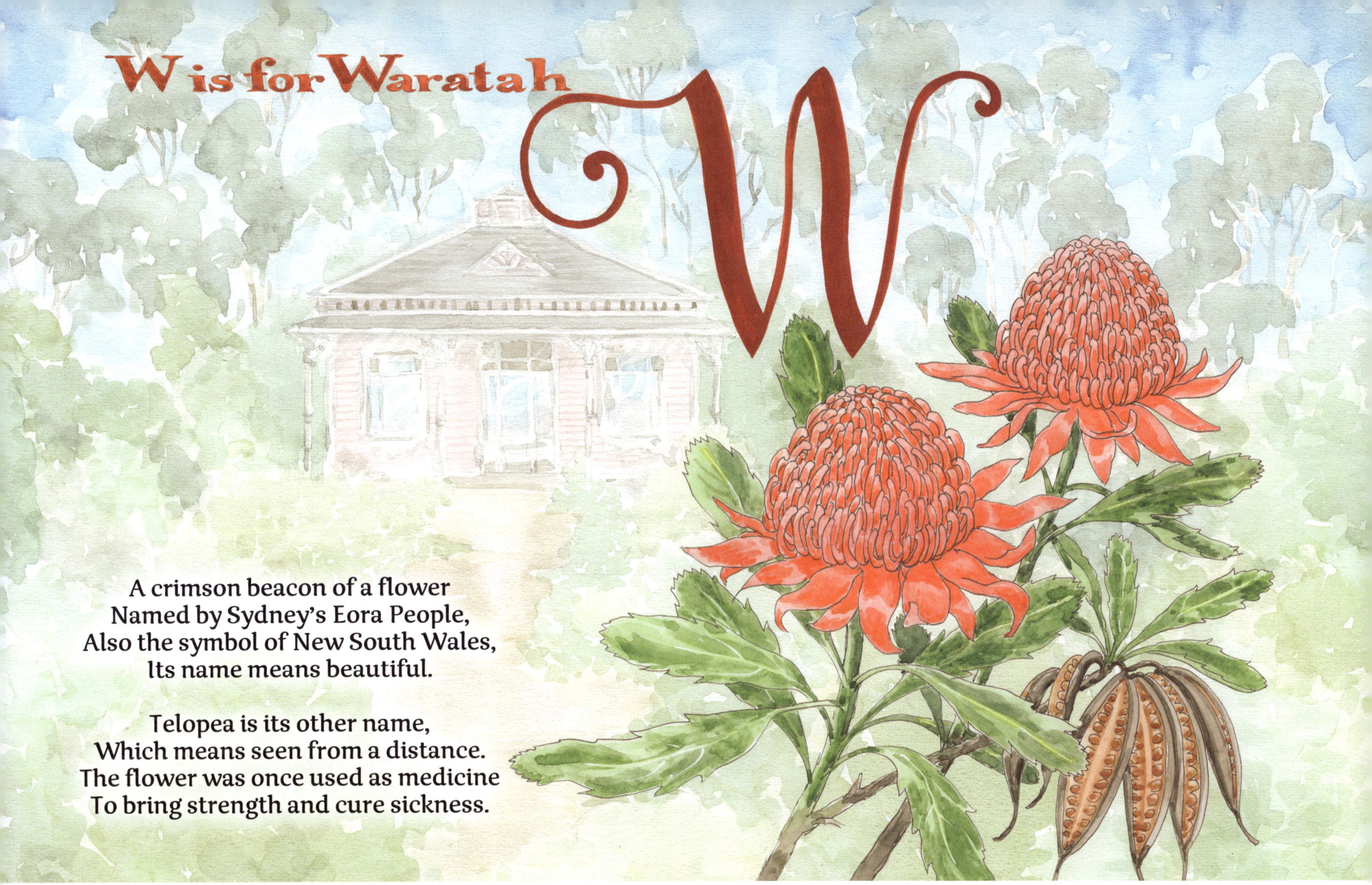

A crimson beacon of a flower
Named by Sydney's Eora People,
Also the symbol of New South Wales,
Its name means beautiful.

Telopea is its other name,
Which means seen from a distance.
The flower was once used as medicine
To bring strength and cure sickness.

Also known as: telopea, and warada (in Dharug language)
Did you know? In the times before the early settlers, Waratahs were said to have been placed in a bowl of water so the sweetness and life of the flower would flow into the water and cure children from disease.

These incredible plants
Have a very long middle spike,
And resin that can be used for tools like spears
Because it's quite glue-like.

Xanthorrhoea can survive wildfires,
In fact, they help the land thrive.
The flowers will burst out after the flames
And provide food, when scarce, for wildlife.

X

X is for Xanthorrhoea

Also known as: grass tree

Did you know? Some Xanthorrhoea can live up to 600 years old. They're known as living fossils because they've been around for thousands of years. The resin they produce bubbles up from the sand after a fire and can be moulded for lots of different uses.

Y is for Yam Daisy

The Yam Daisy is a bush food source,
With roots that can be dug up to eat.
The tubers are then put in a dillybag
And roasted in the earth at high heat.

Digging for tubers is good for the soil,
But when settlers came to farm,
The grazing cattle, sheep and goats
Caused the Daisy a lot of harm.

Also known as: microseris, and murnong (in Woiwurrung language)
Did you know? Yam Daisies are a bit like potatoes. They can be cooked by roasting them in an earth oven.

Z is for Zamia Palm

The palm-like fronds of this plant
Have a giant cone in their midst,
Housing seeds that are poisonous
If you don't know how to handle it.

Some First Nations Australians used it
To poison fish in the creek.
It was also a food source for people
Once processed and soaked for a week.

Also known as: Macrozamia riedlei
Did you know? In March, the mullet would be in the Swan River, which was the same time as the Zamia would flower. Some First Nations Australians would use the nut to stun the fish at this time.

About the Author

After 15 years of a full-on, adventure-packed advertising career, Josephine (Joey) now happily spends her days creating web content for large organisations, writing books and teaching meditation. She also takes every opportunity to go on bushwalks with her family.

This is Joey's first children's book, inspired by Cicely Mary Barker's *Flower Fairies*. Joey felt it was time to bring some of the beauty and interesting facts about Australian flora to children and adults alike — helping them embrace and become intrigued by the secrets of the land.

About the Illustrator

Illustrator Jocelyn Gibson was born in Pretoria, South Africa and attended art school in Johannesburg. She immigrated to the States and lived in Texas and Arizona, before losing her heart to San Francisco and California.

After several years of designing and producing corporate events nationally in the USA, she started her own art and design company and began to focus exclusively on illustration. A lifelong love of plants and gardening became a recurring theme in her work. Jocelyn is also fond of drawing wildlife, birds, humans and "just about everything else!"

In 2019 Jocelyn made a giant leap across the Pacific to join her two brothers in Tasmania. Jocelyn has fallen in love with Tasmania and has a flourishing garden with many native Australian plants and a busy studio filled with creative projects.